For
Teddy, Babby, Bruno
and the gang.

To

....

with love from

....

Katherine Sully and Janet Samuel

PRODUCED FOR CHAD VALLEY TOYS
489-499 Avebury Boulevard,
Central Milton Keynes, MK9 2NW

www.argos.co.uk

ISBN 978-1-4454-3170-3
Batch Code: S22716
Made in Guangzhou, China

Where, Oh Where Is

Huggle Buggle Bear?

Where, oh where is **Huggle Buggle** Bear?
I can't find him anywhere!
He always hides when it's time for bed.
He is such a **funny** bear!

Is he snacking on toast and honey,
Making crumbs with **Babbity Bunny**?

No!
He isn't with
Babbity Bunny.

It's way past **Huggle Buggle**'s bedtime
And I'm feeling very cross.
I can't go to bed without him.
I hope he isn't lost!

Where, oh where is **Huggle Buggle** Bear?
I can't find him anywhere!
He always hides when it's time for bed.
He is such a **silly** bear!

Is he bouncing on his belly,
On the sofa with Ellie Nellie?

No!
He isn't bouncing with
Ellie Nellie.
And he isn't snacking with
Babbity Bunny.

It's way past **Huggle Buggle**'s bedtime
And I'm feeling very sleepy.
I can't go to bed without him,
It's much too dark and creepy.

Where, oh where is **Huggle Buggle** Bear?
I can't find him anywhere!
He always hides when it's time for bed.
He is such a **naughty** bear!

Is he making lots of noise
With Woolly Lamb and the other toys?

No!
He isn't playing with
Woolly Lamb.
He isn't bouncing with
Ellie Nellie.
He isn't snacking with
Babbity Bunny.

It's way past **Huggle Buggle**'s bedtime
And now I'm feeling worried.
I can't go to bed without him.
That would be really horrid.

Where, oh where is **Huggle Buggle** Bear?
I can't find him anywhere!
He always hides when it's time for bed.
He is such a **bothersome** bear.

Is he splashing in the tub,
Blowing bubbles with **Rubadub**?

No!
He isn't splashing with
Rubadub.
He isn't playing with
Woolly Lamb.
He isn't bouncing with
Ellie Nellie.
He isn't snacking with
Babbity Bunny.

It's way past **Huggle Buggle**'s bedtime
And now I'm feeling sad.
I don't want to go to bed without him,
But I think I'd better had...

I know where...
there's Huggle Buggle Bear!
And all the other toys.
I think they must be fast asleep,
So, **sssh!** Don't make a noise!

Night-night!